MARC BROWN

ARTHUR'S PANTS

RED FOX

For all the kids
who insisted on an
underwear book

A Red Fox Book

Published by Random House Children's Books
20 Vauxhall Bridge Road, London SW1V 2SA

A division of The Random House Group Ltd
London Melbourne Sydney Auckland
Johannesburg and agencies throughout the world

Adapted by Marc Brown from a teleplay by Peter Hirsch

1 3 5 7 9 10 8 6 4 2

First published in the United States of America by
Little, Brown and Company and simultaneously in Canada
by Little, Brown and Company (Canada) Ltd 1999

First published in Great Britain by Red Fox 2000

Printed in Hong Kong

www.randomhouse.co.uk

THE RANDOM HOUSE GROUP Limited Reg. No. 954009

ISBN 0 09 941297 7

Binky Barnes was at the board doing a difficult problem.
"That's correct," said Mr Ratburn. "Very good."

Binky cheered, "Yes!" and dropped his chalk. As he bent down, the class heard a loud RRRIPPP!
Everyone laughed, except Mr Ratburn. "Go to the office and ask Ms Tingley to sew them up," he said.

$$\begin{array}{r} 15 \\ \times\ 4 \\ \hline 60 \end{array}$$

$$\begin{array}{r} 30 \\ \times\ 2 \\ \hline 60 \end{array}$$

$$\begin{array}{r} 80 \\ \times\ 2 \\ \hline \end{array}$$

$$\begin{array}{r} 3 \\ \times \end{array}$$

$$10$$

That afternoon in games, when Binky
came up to bat, Arthur thought about Binky in his
underwear and laughed.
During dinner, Mother asked, "Anything interesting
happen at school today?"
Arthur started to laugh.
"What's so funny?" asked D.W.
But Arthur couldn't stop laughing to answer.

The next morning, Arthur woke up late.
He hurried through breakfast and ran most of the way
to school.
"Sorry I'm late, Mr Ratburn! I guess my alarm—"
Everyone burst out laughing.
"Mr Read, being late is one thing," said Mr Ratburn,
"but not wearing any trousers – *that* is quite another!"
Arthur looked down – and screamed!

Arthur's scream woke him up.
Wow, he thought, *what a horrible dream!*

In school, the class watched a science film. "The amoeba is a single-celled life form . . ." Arthur's eyelids began to droop.

Suddenly, an amoeba that looked a lot like Arthur appeared on the screen. Its trousers fell down, showing its pants.

"Help!" cried Arthur-Amoeba. "I need my trousers!"
All the other amoebas started to laugh.

Arthur-Amoeba was too embarrassed to move. Then
he felt someone shaking him.
"Wake up, Arthur!" said Buster. "The film's over."

At lunch, Arthur didn't feel like eating.
"What should I do, Buster? Every time I go to sleep, I'm in my pants!"
"Try staying awake," Buster suggested. "You can't dream if you don't sleep."

That night, Arthur tried some tricks to stay awake.

Old MacDonald had a farm...

But as hard as he tried,
Arthur just couldn't.

"I'll get you, Verminator . . . After . . . I take . . . a
little nap."

In Arthur's dream, the Verminator was torturing the class by scratching his claws on the blackboard. Hearing cries for help, Bionic Arthur rushed to the rescue!

But as he entered the classroom to take on the Verminator, everyone started laughing.

"My trousers!" Arthur gasped as he woke up with a start. "Rise and shine, Mr Fancy Pants," said D.W. "They're right here. Mom says you'd better shake a leg or you'll be late for school!"

Arthur asked Buster for some emergency advice on
the way to school.
"It even happens when I'm a superhero!" he exclaimed.
"I can't stay awake forever. I'm doomed!"
"Maybe you should sleep in your trousers," said Buster.
"That way you won't have to worry about putting
them on."

That night, D.W. came into Arthur's room.
"Why are you wearing your trousers to bed?" she asked.
"Because . . . ah . . . that way I can be ready for school faster," he said quickly.

"I'm going to ask Mom if I can sleep in my clothes, too,"
D.W. said. "And maybe my coat and boots. Mom?!"
Arthur sighed and changed into his pyjama trousers.

The next day, Arthur was more worried than ever.
"What if people find out about my pant problem?"
he asked Buster. "They'll call me names, and then
I'll have to change schools . . ."
"Don't worry," said Buster. "Your secret is safe with me."

At lunch the following day, Arthur sat with Francine and Muffy. They looked at him and started to giggle.
"What's so funny?" Arthur asked.
"Do you have your trousers on?" asked Francine.
"Better make sure!"

Arthur checked. He was wearing trousers.
He moved to another table.
"I heard about your nightmares," said the Brain, "so I
got out a couple of books on dreams. Apparently, you
have a pathological fear of embarrassment . . ."

Arthur got up to find Buster.

"Buster!" cried Arthur. "You told everyone about my
underwear dreams!"
"Not everyone," replied Buster. "Only a few people."
"Buster, how could you?"
"Well, I couldn't help you. I needed some advice."
"This is so embarrassing!" said Arthur.

When Arthur turned to run out of the cafeteria,
his trouser pocket got caught.

RRRIPPP!

Everyone in the cafeteria began to laugh.
Arthur couldn't move.
But Binky grabbed two trays to cover him.
"Quick!" he whispered. "Into the kitchen!"

Mrs MacGrady wrapped her apron around Arthur and got out a needle and thread.

"I'm sorry," Buster said. "I shouldn't have told anyone."

"It's OK," said Arthur sadly. "You were just trying to help. The hard part will be telling my parents that I have to change schools."

Mrs MacGrady handed Arthur his trousers.

"Thanks," said Arthur. "Is there a back door?"

"Afraid not," said Mrs MacGrady. "But do you know the old saying, 'A banana without its peel is still a banana'?"

"Huh?" said Arthur and Buster.

"It means people get embarrassed all the time," Binky explained.

"But you're still Arthur," said Mrs MacGrady. "A clever, kind young man – with or without your trousers."

Arthur smiled.

A few days later, Arthur met Buster at the Sugar Bowl.
"Well, no more underwear nightmares!" Arthur said.
"That's great!" said Buster. "I never thought that ripping
your trousers in the cafeteria would be the thing to
cure you."
As they stood up to leave, Arthur looked at Buster
and frowned.
"Uh, Buster . . . I think you forgot something."

Buster woke up with a scream.
"Uh-oh," he sighed. "Here we go again!"